Caroline Pitcher studied English and European Literature
Wa vick L niversity. She later became a primary school teacher
Lo lon d is now a freelance writer. Her previous titles include
V , ald and the Pelican and *Jo's Storm*. *The Snow Whale*,
b for Frances Lincoln, was one of ten titles shortlisted
C en's Book Award. Caroline lives in Belper, Derbyshire.

rew up in south-west England and studied illustration
v. She has worked in magazine publishing and has
ards for Greenpeace, Amnesty International and Oxfam.
Storm, was written by Caroline Pitcher, and they also
on *The Snow Whale*. Jackie lives in Dyfed, Wales.

For Elizabeth - *C.P. and J.M.*

The Time of the Lion copyright © Frances Lincoln Limited 1998
Text copyright © Caroline Pitcher 1998
Illustrations copyright © Jackie Morris 1998

First published in Great Britain in 1998 by
Frances Lincoln Limited, 4 Torriano Mews
Torriano Avenue, London NW5 2RZ

British Library Cataloguing in Publication Data
available on request

ISBN 0-7112-1194-9 - hardback
ISBN 0-7112-1338-0 - paperback

Printed in Hong Kong
9 8 7 6 5 4 3 2 1

THE TIME
OF THE LION

Caroline Pitcher

Illustrated by
Jackie Morris

FRANCES LINCOLN

One night, while his village slept, Joseph heard a ROAR thunderclap across the wide savannah.

   "Who's that?" he whispered.

   "It's the Lion," said his father.

   "Can I meet him?" asked Joseph.

   "No," said his father. "It's not time."

But Joseph thought it *was* time.

So next morning he went looking for the Lion, past the wildebeest at the waterhole, round the elephants, zig-zag through the zebras, beyond the buffalo.

All he could see was grass and sky.

"I don't believe there is a lion!" cried Joseph.

Then a ROAR thunderclapped across the wide savannah and Joseph saw the sun racing towards him. Its great head streamed with gold. It sprang on paws as big as drums, and its amber eyes glittered so that Joseph feared they'd burn him up there and then.

But Joseph stood his ground.

He said, "I didn't know a lion could be so big."

The Lion said, "I didn't know a boy could be so small. You're like my smallest cub, my little lion. Mmmmm... I could knock you down with one swipe of my paw and toss you to my family for tea."

"Mmmmm..." said Joseph. "I could tell my father you are stealing his cattle, and he would come after you with guns and spears."

"But you won't, will you?" growled the Lion.

"No. And you won't feed me to your family, will you?" said Joseph.

"Not today," said the Lion. "Now Joseph, I am sleepy. Come and rest with me."

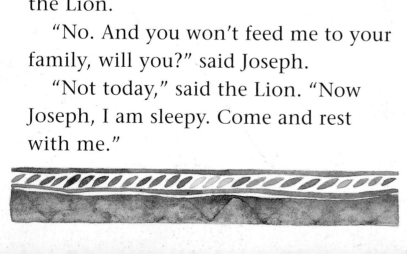

Joseph walked beside the Lion to a grassy den.

The Lion yawned and sprawled and began to purr a mighty purr, like water gurgling in a giant plughole.

Joseph leaned against the Lion's sand-dune side. He said, "Our sorcerers try to turn themselves into lions by magic. Now I know why! You are wonderful, King Lion."

They slept, and when they woke, the heat of the day shimmered at the edge of the savannah.

"I'll walk you home to your village, to keep you safe," said the Lion. "Danger is not always where you think, Joseph. There are hungry hyenas and lean leopards, rampaging elephants and easy-running cheetahs."

"And lions," laughed Joseph.

"And most of all, men," growled the Lion.

They strolled together under the purple African skies until they reached the walls of Joseph's village.

"Remember, I am always here, just out of your sight," purred the Lion, and he melted away in a cloud of gold-dust.

Every noon-time after that, Joseph stole away to meet the Lion, past the wildebeest at the water-hole, round the elephants, zig-zag through the zebras, beyond the buffalo.

He sheltered by the Lion's side and heard the Lion's great heart beat like the heart of the savannah, just under his cheek, and together they watched the lion-cubs play.

The Lion said, "Your father has his family, Joseph. I have my pride. See my brave, hard-working lioness?" He yawned. "See my cubs? I love to roll them over and bat them softly with my paw! The smaller, the better."

Joseph and the Lion played too - very carefully.

But Joseph never told his father, because his father had said it was not time.

Then the traders came.

"What can we buy from you?" they asked Joseph's father. "We will pay well for anything you make, and sell it to the tourists. And," they whispered, "we pay *very* well for lion cubs. The smaller, the better."

Joseph's heart leapt in his chest like a gazelle.

His father replied, "We have beads and baskets." He looked down at Joseph with glittering eyes. "But do we know where there are little lion cubs, boy? The smaller, the better?"

"No, Father," cried Joseph, and his face grew hot with the lie.

"If there are cubs, then we will find them," said the traders. "We will hunt them down and take them away, far across the sea."

And Joseph watched in horror as they set out across the savannah.

At noon-time, Joseph ran past
the wildebeest at the water-hole,
round the elephants, zig-zag through
the zebras, beyond the buffalo.

He saw the traders, hunting in
the scrub.

He saw his father running easy
as a cheetah, back to the village.

Then he saw the Lion rise at
the edge of the savannah like a dark
sun, alone!

"My father has betrayed the cubs!"
cried Joseph, and he wept for all
the lions in the world.

Later, in the cool of the day, the traders returned.

"We have beadwork and baskets and fine cloth to sell," Joseph's father said to the traders. "Our pots are the smoothest you can buy. The tourists will give you a good price for them. But don't touch those big ones at the back! They are no good - they're far too rough and scratchy."

From the doorway, Joseph watched his father go into a huddle with the traders. Money and goods changed hands. Then the traders left, trundling off across the wide savannah.

Joseph hid his face in shame.

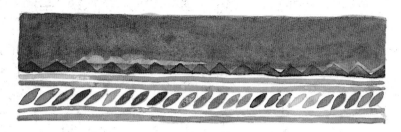

That night, while the village slept, Joseph went looking for his friend. The stars glittered like the eyes of lions, watching him steal across the tawny land.

He waited.

No ROAR. No sun. No Lion.

Nothing.

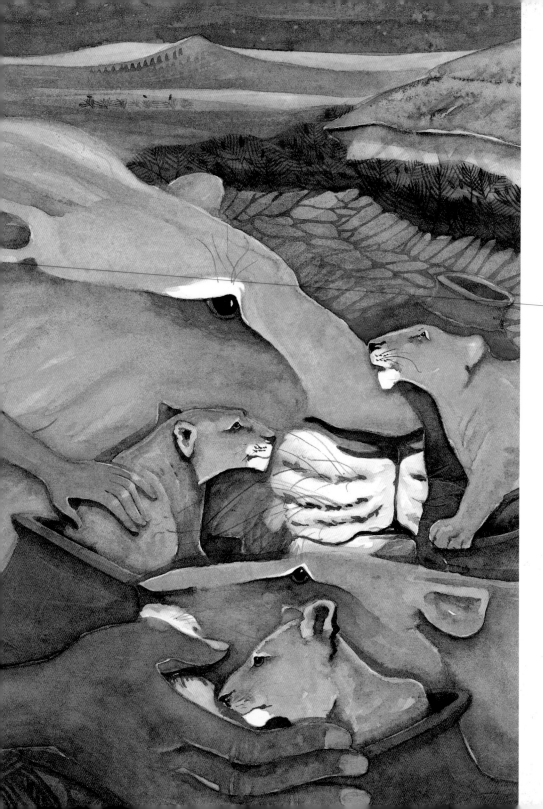

Joseph wandered back towards the village.

When he reached the wall, a shadow spread over him like smoke, and someone cried out, "Joseph!", shattering the great bowl of night.

It was his father.

And from the shadows sprang the Lion and Lioness, as if spelled there by a sorcerer!

"Don't kill the Lion, I beg you, Father," pleaded Joseph, sheltering the Lion's savannah side.

His father smiled.

"Why should I kill him, Joseph? I am giving him back what is his. I kept his cubs from danger, just as he kept you safe."

"Father, aren't you cross with me?" said Joseph. "You said it wasn't time to meet the Lion."

"You were right and I was wrong, Joseph. It *was* time," said his father. "Lion, when I was a boy, I was your father's friend, and I spent my noon-times with him. The Time of the Lion is more precious than gold."

Joseph looked up at his father in amazement. Had this man once been a small boy, and learned from lions?

The Lion nodded, so that his mighty mane shook, gold-dust caught in moonshine.

Then he was gone, into the night.

Now at night-time, while the village sleeps, and Joseph hears a ROAR thunderclap across the wide savannah, he understands what it says:

The Time of the Lion is more precious than gold.
Let it be always the Time of the Lion.

OTHER PICTURE BOOKS IN PAPERBACK FROM FRANCES LINCOLN

The Snow Whale
Caroline Pitcher
Illustrated by Jackie Morris

One November morning, when the hills are hump-backed with snow,
Laurie and Leo decide to build a snow whale. As they shovel, pat and polish it
out of the hill, the whale gradually takes on a life of its own.

Shortlisted for the Children's Book Award 1997

Suitable for National Curriculum English – Reading, Key Stage 1
Scottish Guidelines English Language – Reading, Levels A and B
ISBN 0-7112-1093-4   £4.99

Rainbow Bird
Eric Maddern
Illustrated by Adrienne Kennaway

"I'm boss for Fire," growls rough, tough Crocodile Man, and he keeps the rest
of the world cold and dark, until one day clever Bird Woman sees her opportunity
and seizes it. An Aboriginal fire myth, lit with glowing illustrations.

Suitable for National Curriculum English – Reading, Key Stage 1
Scottish Guidelines English Language – Reading, Levels A and B
ISBN 0-7112-0898-0   £4.99

Growing Pains
Jenny Stow

Poor baby Shukudu! It's hard trying to be a rhinoceros when you have no horns.
"Horns take time to grow," says his mother. How Shukudu learns patience
and gains his heart's desire is portrayed with warmth and humour by Jenny Stow.

Suitable for National Curriculum English – Reading, Key Stage 1
Scottish Guidelines English Language – Reading, Levels B and C
ISBN 0-7112-1036-5   £4.99

Frances Lincoln titles are available from all good bookshops.
Prices are correct at time of publication, but may be subject to change.